P9-DWN-594

GOOD DOG, CARL

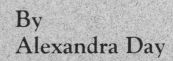

By
Alexandra Day

To H.D., who has never let us forget about Ponies

SIMON & SCHUSTER BOOKS FOR YOUNG READERS
An imprint of Simon & Schuster Children's Publishing Division
1230 Avenue of the Americas, New York, New York 10020
Copyright © 1985 by Alexandra Day
All rights reserved, including the right of reproduction in whole or in part in any form.
SIMON & SCHUSTER BOOKS FOR YOUNG READERS is a trademark of Simon & Schuster, Inc.
For information about special discounts for bulk purchases, please contact Simon & Schuster Special Sales at
1-866-506-1949 or business@simonandschuster.com.
The Simon & Schuster Speakers Bureau can bring authors to your live event.
For more information or to book an event, contact the Simon & Schuster Speakers Bureau at
1-866-248-3049 or visit our website at www.simonspeakers.com.
Manufactured in China
0610 KWO
2 4 6 8 10 9 7 5 3 1
CIP data for this book is available from the Library of Congress.
ISBN 978-1-4424-1660-4

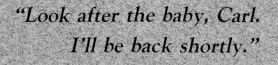

"Look after the baby, Carl.
I'll be back shortly."

"Good dog, Carl!"

A salute to the creator of Münchener Bilderbogen No. 1001,
and thanks to Molly Myers and Toby for their sitting talent.

The paintings for this book were executed in egg tempera.
Color separations by Photolitho, AG, Gossau/Zurich, Switzerland.
Printed and bound in China.